Far-Fetched Pets

YOUR PET KANGAROO

By Bobbie Hamsa

Illustrations by Tom Dunnington

Consultant:
James P. Rowan
Keeper, Small Mammal House
Lincoln Park Zoo, Chicago

Ideals Publishing Corp.
Milwaukee, Wisconsin

To John, Kris, Angela and Dom

CAUTION
Far-fetched pets can live only in your imagination. So don't ask for one for your birthday or Christmas. Go to the zoo or visit the library. There you can learn more about your favorite far-fetched pet.

Printed and bound in U.S.A.
Published simultaneously in Canada.
Published by Ideals Publishing Corporation
Milwaukee, Wisconsin 53201
ISBN 0-8249-8030-1

This is a kangaroo.
A Great Gray Kangaroo.
Pretend that she is your pet.

HOPPY ?

KANGA

MARTHA

Matilda?

Roo?

She has soft, wooly fur.

Big back feet.

Little front feet.

A built-in pouch.

And a thick, thumpy tail as long as your bed.

What will you name your pet kangaroo?

CARE AND FEEDING OF YOUR PET

Kangaroos eat vegetables, tender grass, and leaves.

Delicious spinach, broccoli, and cauliflower.

Kangaroos are called grazers.

That means they feed on grass and low-lying plants.

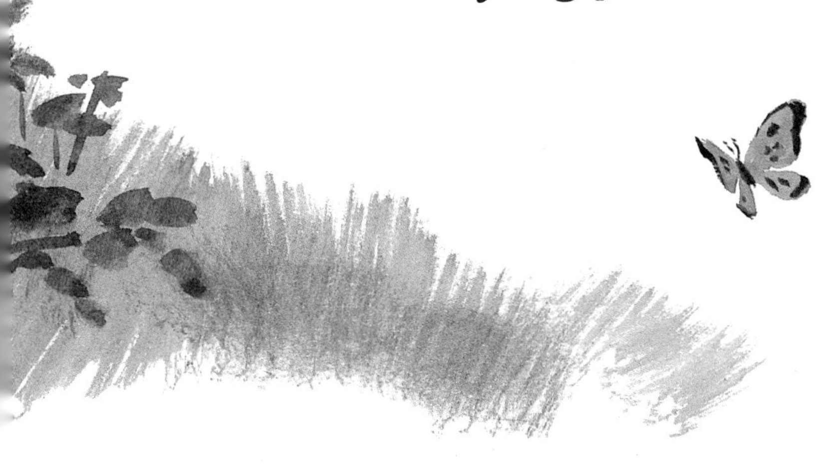

Feed your pet five times a day.

Before you go to bed.

Again at midnight.

Again at 3:00 A.M.

And before you go to school.

Then give her peanuts, alfalfa, and mashed oat mush when you get home again.

Your pet is rather shy.
She will need her own quiet spot.
Perhaps there's room under your bed?
Or in the guest room closet?
If not, build a giant dog house.
Or borrow your father's sleeping bag.
(It will remind her of her mother's pouch.)

A baby kangaroo is called a joey (even if it's a girl).

If she's just been born, she'll fit in a tablespoon.

But once she starts growing, she shoots up.

By the time you're ready for college, she'll be about as tall as you.

Have fun with your pet.
She loves a playful boxing match
(no hitting below the pouch).
She likes dodge ball and hopscotch.

No one is better at jumping rope.

Or hurdles. Or sand pits.

So make sure she's on your team if you ever enter a track meet.

Your pet can walk, but very slowly.
She jumps where she wants to go.
So keep her out of low places.
Like subways and attics,
tents, tunnels, and prairie dog holes.
Or she'll get blisters on her head.

TRAINING

A kangaroo can be very useful
(especially if your Dad's a mailman).
She can help your brother on his
paper route . . .
help you deliver Valentines and
May baskets . . .
sell things door-to-door . . .
bring in the groceries . . .
take out the cat . . .
and carry dishes to the table and back.
Almost without breaking any.

She can hold bubble gum cards . . .
rock collections . . .
Tooth Fairy teeth . . .
yarn, leaves, magazines, doll clothes.
And your most very valuable junk.

5

She's more than willing to carry picnic stuff.

And she makes the world's first really portable wastebasket.

She can carry your gym shoes and books to school . . .

p.j.'s and toothbrush to slumber parties.

She can give you a warm ride anywhere on any cold morning . . .

and boy, can she hold a bundle on Halloween!

She can hide a report card that's *not* so great . . .

Christmas or Hanukkah presents that *are* . . .

and YOU when Mom says
"Who ate all the cookies?"

Train her to jump you over puddles . . .
over traffic . . .
away from bullies . . .
and up long flights of stairs . . .
to help you peek over circus fences . . .
and catch home runs before they leave the park.

She can make pancake batter.

Mix orange juice.

Scramble eggs.

(All at the same time if you're in a hurry for breakfast).

She can turn milk into malts . . .
cream into butter . . .
and shake up the dice for Monopoly games.

She's a pretty strong kicker, too.
For when the elevator doors get stuck . . .
or your soccer team needs help . . .

or when you want to practice your karate lesson . . .

or rearrange your room . . .

and if Dad ever wants to move the rock garden to the other side of the yard.

These are only a few of the things your pet can do.

Can you think of more?

BEST
PET

If you take good care of her,
your kangaroo will live maybe 18 years.
And you'll say she's the best pet you ever had.

Facts about your pet Great Gray Kangaroo (Macropus major)

Size at birth (weight & height): 3/4 of an inch long, about 1 ounce in weight

Number of newborn: 1 (occasionally 2)

Average size when grown (weight & height): 6 to 7 feet tall, up to 200 pounds for an adult male—females are a little smaller

Type of food eaten: grass and low-lying vegetation

Amount of food eaten (daily): probably amounts to about a bushel of vegetation

Expected lifespan: up to 18 years

Names—male: Boomer
female: Doe
young: Joey
group: Mob

Where found: Grasslands and open forests in eastern and southeastern Australia

About the Author:

Bobbie Hamsa was born and raised in Nebraska, far away from any far-fetched pets. She has a Bachelor of Arts Degree in English Literature from the University of Nebraska. She is married and has a son, John.

Bobbie Hamsa is an advertising copywriter in Omaha. She writes print, radio, and television copy for a full range of accounts, including Mutual of Omaha's "Wild Kingdom," the five-time Emmy Award winning wild animal series and sometime resource for far-fetched pets.

About the Artist:

Tom Dunnington divides his time between book illustration and wildlife painting. He has done many books for Childrens Press, as well as working on textbooks, and is a regular contributor to "Highlights for Children." Tom lives in Oak Park, Illinois.